WANDI'S LITTLE VOICE

ELLEN BANDA-AAKU

WANDI'S LITTLE VOICE

ELLEN BANDA-AAKU

Gadsden Publishers

Gadsden Publishers
P.O. Box 32581, Lusaka, Zambia

© Ellen Banda-Aaku 2004

First published by Macmillan Education Ltd in 2004
This edition published by
Gadsden Publishers in 2021

All rights reserved. No part of this publication may be reproduced, stored in a retrievable system or transmitted in any form by any means without permission in writing from the publishers.

Cover photograph by Chabala Nsomi.

ISBN: 978 9982 24 1250

WANDI IN MATELO

To keep my dress out of the way, I've hitched it up and tucked it into the elastic around the leg holes of my underwear. Wandi! Wandi! Wandi! My team mates, spurred on by Leah, my best friend, cheer me on. We're in the middle of the road playing 'chicken-in-the-den'.

That's what we call it at my school. Here in Matelo shanty town we simply call it 'game'. I duck, jump and swerve around the ball that's swishing past me, to and fro, as the other team members try to knock me out. I'm last in the game. My team mates have been knocked out and I can tell from the way they're hurling the ball at me that the other team is getting frustrated that I've lasted so long. The cheers keep me going. Each time the ball whizzes past me I taunt the other team by making funny faces at them. Suddenly the cheering stops. Almost simultaneously, I realize the ball isn't coming at me any more. Angela, a girl in the other team, is holding the ball and staring straight past me. I turn to follow her gaze. I freeze. Charging towards me, waving her arms around vigorously, is my mother!

****

My name is Wandi. My Granny-da, which is what I call my grandmother on my father's side, gave me the name. She had seven sons and four grandsons before I came along. My mother says Granny-da didn't have any daughters because she's too mean and cruel. However, Granny-da believed forces other than nature were at play. So she recruited her local medicine man to intervene. The medicine man apparently uncovered a curse that had been placed on Granny-da by one of my father's paternal aunties. No female child would descend from Granny-da as long as the curse was in place. By the time Granny-da discovered this it was too late for her. She was too old to have any more children. Nonetheless, she begged the medicine man to lift the curse so she could at least have granddaughters. At the time my father had recently married my mother, and was therefore assumed to be next in line to produce a grandchild. He was made to sacrifice a white chicken to appease the spirit of his deceased auntie. My father is a medical doctor who doesn't believe in the supernatural. So the fact that Granny-da convinced him to partake in the whole ritual is, according to my mother, a miracle. Anyway, as it happened, my mother gave birth to me. Granny-da gave herself credit for my being a girl. She staked her claim by naming me 'Wandi', which literally means 'mine'.

My mother and Granny-ma, which is what I call my grandmother on my mother's side, were furious with Granny-da, though I believe they were wise enough not to challenge her. You see, Granny-da is a tall, dark, fierce-looking woman who has a reputation for meddling in witchcraft. No one crosses her. In her village, she's rumoured to be a witch. I'm her favourite grandchild, for obvious reasons, but I'm terrified of her. Whenever I'm alone in her company, I clam up in terror as all the stories Beauty, our house girl, and Leah have told me about witchcraft fill my mind. Granny-da is oblivious to my fears: she dotes on me, indulging me with gifts, praise and endless folk stories. No matter how hard I try to overcome my fear, the best I can do is respond to my grandmother with tepid enthusiasm. I feel guilty for being frightened of Granny-da because I don't really believe she's a witch. I think people say she is because of her undying faith in medicine men. There was a time she spent her days frequenting medicine men for various ailments at a huge cost to her sons. Until Uncle Robert, my father's next elder brother, put a stop to it. He offered to drive Granny-da on one of her regular visits to one of her regular medicine men. On arrival, much to Granny-da's horror, Uncle Robert grabbed the medicine man and threatened to beat him up if he continued to diagnose problems and prescribe costly solutions for Granny-da's imagined ailments. According to Uncle Robert, the spectacle took place in front of all the other patients, who no doubt knew Granny-da. Ever since, Granny-da has kept the details of her ailments and trips to medicine men to herself!

****

It's an hour since my mother dragged me off the street. I'm sitting on the verandah of our four-bedroomed bungalow. It all seems to have happened a long time ago. Maybe it's because I've endured so much in the past hour. By the time my mother reached me, Leah and all the other children had scattered away to a safe distance. My mother grabbed me by the ear and led me home along the pot-holed roads, lined with wooden poles that once supported street lights that worked. We weaved our way through the small derelict houses of Matelo, towards the main road. To get to the main road we had to cross the huge ditch that runs around the outskirts of Matelo. Apparently in the colonial days a high wire fence ran along the ditch to cordon off the area in order to keep black people out. Or in, depending on which side of the fence you were standing. My mother was ranting and raving as we marched home. She stopped briefly to negotiate the make shift bridge over the ditch. Two parallel wooden planks were wedged into the red soil on either side of the ditch. Once across the bridge we ascended towards the main road that divided the shanty township of Matelo from Shrublands suburb where I live.

My mother carried on shouting but I was so frightened of the fate that awaited me at home, I didn't take in most of what she was saying. In any case I didn't have to listen to her words; I guessed she was forbidding me for the umpteenth time from playing in Matelo. My mother didn't want me mixing with the children from or going anywhere near the place.

How could I explain to her that Matelo was an experience! In Matelo children were free to play - timeless, boundary-less, fearless, play! Where else would we get away with converting a road to a playing field? In Matelo the few cars that drove along 'our' road, drove around us.

No one watched us like hawks as we played. No one interrupted playtime because it was time for homework, afternoon tea or a bath.

The streets of Matelo are always busy because no one sits indoors. The houses are very small and usually so many people live in them there's hardly any space to sit indoors. Everyone goes about business outdoors. Women cook, bathe children, and wash clothes. Men listen to their radios, play drafts, and discuss politics under the shade of trees. I knew my mother wouldn't understand or approve my explanations so I listened to my little voice when it asked me to keep quiet.

My mother probably wouldn't even have heard me. She was very agitated. Something else was up. I couldn't understand why she had come to find me personally. On the odd occasion in the past when she gets home before me, my mother has sent Beauty to find me. Beauty and I would normally concoct a story about where I was so my mother wouldn't know I had crossed the ditch into Matelo.

My mother must have read my mind.

"Wandi, why do you insist on going to Matelo?" she panted heavily as we walked. "Look at how dirty you are. Auntie Betty will be here any minute!"

Everything fell into place. My mother was horrified at the thought of Auntie Betty seeing me covered in red dust. Or worse still, she feared Auntie Betty might find out I played in Matelo. It was Auntie Betty's impending visit that had my mother desperate enough to venture out into Matelo. We crossed the main road and jogged the rest of the way home in silence. On the other side of the road we were in a different world. The houses in Shrublands suburb are surrounded by pretty fenced hedges and high walls. The tarred roads are neatly paved and lined with working street lights. Typically the streets were quiet. In Shrublands one hardly sees pedestrians. Once in a while a car drives in or out of the security manned gates. Shrublands residential area was for 'whites only' before independence. Since independence, it's mixed. My father say's we won't really be independent until more black people are able to move out of places like Matelo and into areas like Shrublands. I understand what he means, but his theory contradicts my Social Studies teacher who insists we are all independent.

As we approached our front gate I knew my mother was praying none of our neighbours was watching. She exhaled as we walked through our gate. My mother's Fiat was the only car in the drive. We made it home before Auntie Betty arrived.

MY MOTHER

Granny-ma once told me that realizing that one's parents are normal human beings with faults is a sign of growing up. I didn't say anything, but I remember thinking back to when I first realized my mother had a problem. I was seven years old. My mother's problem stems from Granny-ma's younger sister, Auntie Betty. She's actually my grandmother but I call her Auntie because that's what everyone else calls her. I've never understood why as a young girl my mother was sent to live with Auntie Betty, even though both my grandparents were alive. I'm not sure what her life was like living with her Auntie. But I know it has left my mother scarred for life. She sees herself and those close to her through Auntie Betty's eyes. Whenever something good happens to my mother she won't rest until Auntie Betty hears of it. It's as if she always has a point to prove to Auntie Betty. And when Auntie Betty is due a visit, my mother cleans the house spotless. She has everyone in the household in their church clothes. She then drills us, my father included, on how to be on our best behaviour.

However, what disturbs me most is that my mother goes much further than presenting a clean picture of her household and her family to Auntie Betty. She tells Auntie Betty lots of stories, some of which are untrue. Since it's not really acceptable for children to question grown-ups, I kept quiet about it for a while. It nagged me, particularly when my mother told me or my younger brother Junior off for not telling the truth. One day my mother smacked me hard for lying that I had finished doing my homework.

My behind smarting, I ran out of the kitchen into the hall and shouted at her "If it's wrong to lie how come you lied to Auntie Betty that Daddy had gone to England when you knew he was in the north of the country?"

From where I was standing I saw my mother stiffen; I had caught her off guard. I expected her to come after me. When she didn't, I realized I had put her in an awkward position. For some strange reason, though I knew my question was justified, I regretted having opened my mouth. My mother looked ashamed and I didn't like seeing her that way. I hovered by the kitchen doorway unsure of what to do.

"Wandi." My mother lowered her voice which was unlike her when she's angry. "Have I not told you not to listen to adults' conversations?"

At this point, I probably should have reminded my mother that I happened to be sitting in the living room with the adults when she told her lie. But I decided to listen to the little voice that asked me to shut up.

"Have you forgotten your manners?" my mother asked. "I'll tell your Granny-ma."

The magic words were spoken. My mother knew how I adored my grandmother and how much I went out of my way to be in her good books. By bringing Granny-ma into the picture my mother knew I would never question her on the subject again. She was right, but I noticed she didn't say anything obviously untrue to Auntie Betty when I was around after that. I didn't challenge her again; I understood the rules. No one was allowed in lie, except my mother to Auntie Betty.

As soon as we got into the house my mother ordered me to the bathroom. "I'll come and wash your hair," she announced. I feared the worst, justifiably, because mother combed my kinky hair with an unnecessarily small-toothed comb and then she shampooed it three times. After my bath, as I changed into the baby-pink dress my mother insisted I wear, the smell of hot metal and burning hair wafted through the room. My mother was preparing the hot comb. I finished dressing and joined her in the kitchen. She parted my damp hair into sections and smeared pomade into my scalp. I then endured fifteen minutes of having my hair stretched from the roots to the split ends. The combination of water from my damp hair and the sulphur and pomade sizzled down to my scalp making me cringe in pain. I didn't protest, I knew my mother. This was all part of my punishment for going to Matelo.

The pain was so unbearable that I took comfort in a silent prayer: *"Dear God, this woman can't be my mother. Please send my real mother to rescue me."*

****

I've been sitting on the verandah for an hour and a half and there's still no sign of Auntie Betty. I have to admit my straightened hair looks nice tied in a single bun on the top of my head.

I can see Leah through the mulberry trees, playing in her garden. But I daren't move. My mother left instructions for me to sit and wait for Auntie Betty. "If you move about and sweat, your hair will shrink. Then I'll have to stretch it all over again!" Her threat works wonders. I sit glued to my chair.

I miss Granny-ma. If she were here, I know she would be sitting right here next to me. But

I know its wishful thinking. Granny-ma and Auntie Betty don't particularly get along. I know it's not coincidence that Auntie Betty has never paid us a visit when Granny-ma is around.

Granny-ma is my favourite relation. She lives with us for some months of the year. Ever since my grandfather died she has no permanent home of her own. She rotates between her children's homes. I love it when she comes to stay with us because she's the one person I can tell everything. Well, almost everything. She knows my secrets and she tells me hers. Because Granny-ma is soft spoken and calm many people mistake her for quiet, but she isn't. Granny-ma has a lot to say, particularly about her six children. Auntie Freda is the eldest of Granny-ma's children. She is so like Granny-ma in many ways. She lives on a farm in another town so we don't see much of her. Auntie Freda's children are all grown up so Granny-ma spends most of her time with her. Auntie Aggie is Granny-ma's second child. Third is Uncle Mark. He's my favourite Uncle. He's forever cheerful. Whenever he comes to visit us he has the household in stitches. Even my father, who is usually ill at ease in company other than his own, enjoys Uncle Mark's company. My mother is Granny-ma's fourth child. She was the youngest child for seven years until Auntie Natasha came along followed by Uncle Kasuli two years later. I often ask Granny-ma how a calm person like her can produce characters like Uncle Mark and my mother. She replies with an African proverb: 'The womb is a jungle'

AUNTIE BETTY

The sound of a car beep at the gate announces the arrival of Auntie Betty. I'm not sure whether to run inside to alert my mother or to greet the visitors on my own. I can't decide quickly enough so I'm still standing on the verandah when the Mercedes rolls to a stop at the front of our flower-lined drive. Auntie Betty steps out of the car, followed closely behind by Auntie Esther, her half- sister and protégée.

"Wandi." Auntie Betty holds her arms out to me. "Look how you've grown. How are you?"

I walk down the verandah steps and shuffle hesitantly into her arms. She's wearing her trademark afro wig under her scarf. The green and brown tie-dye head tie she's wearing matches her wrap.

"I'm fine Grand-ma." At least I've remembered to call her Grand-ma.

Auntie Betty steps back to look at me. Then she shakes my hand as though the hug was not enough. I oblige, holding out my right hand and curtseying as a customary sign of respect. I can tell both women are impressed. So far, so good.

I shake Auntie Esther's hand. She utters the same words of greeting as her half sister.

For a rare moment, I find myself agreeing with my mother. She always says Auntie Esther imitates Auntie Betty. Apparently Auntie Esther adores Auntie Betty.

"Hello." My mother's over-cheerful voice interrupts my greeting ritual. My mother is a pretty, small-built woman. She takes great care in her personal appearance and surroundings. I can see she's tried hard to look causal today but her strong perfume and bright red lips give her away. She hurries across the verandah and down the steps into Auntie Betty's waiting arms. "It's good to see you Auntie. Welcome. Did you have a safe journey?"

"Tanya you look as good as always!" Auntie Betty exclaims.

"You do look well," Auntie Esther imitates her.

I watch the spectacle bemused. I can't fathom the pretence of it all. I know for a fact my mother and Auntie Betty do not like one another, but for some reason they pretend.

Auntie Betty has not forgotten about me as I hoped. She takes hold of my hand as my mother leads the entourage through the spotlessly clean hall and into the living room. Auntie Betty makes herself comfortable on the olive green three-seater sofa and gestures at me to sit beside her. I'm stuck.

"Where is your brother?" Auntie Betty asks after my younger brother and only sibling.

"He went with his father to the clinic this morning," my mother says before I can reply. "They don't get many patients on Saturday's so junior goes along to keep his father company."

I know Junior has never been to the clinic with my father on a Saturday but I obey my little voice. Junior has ringworm on his scalp. My mother insisted that he accompany my father to the clinic even though my father said it wasn't necessary. At the time I couldn't see why my mother was so determined that Junior should go with my father. Now I realize she didn't want Auntie Betty to see him with ringworm.

I smile to myself. I'm pleased Junior has ringworm because it's given me something to tease him about. Junior is always provoking me over one thing or another. Up until recently, Junior and I settled our scores physically. I preferred it that way because I always had the upper hand and managed to shut him up for a while. Our last fight was over a comic of mine he was reading. When I asked to have it back, he held it out to me then withdrew it as I reached across to take it. He laughed at me for falling for his prank, which irritated me. I chased him out of the bedroom through the hall and into the kitchen where I thumped him on the back as he slowed down to maneuver past the kitchen table. Anticipating his response, I tried to run away but sensing he would catch me before I reached the sanctuary of my room, I decided to face him. We locked arms as we both struggled to get away without being hit. I summed up all my strength to push Junior away but to my surprise he didn't budge. My heartbeat quickened as I realised Junior was holding up, he didn't look as tired as I felt.

He smirked menacingly. "I can beat you now." Caught up in his gloating, Junior momentarily lost his concentration. I shook him off and fled. I slammed my bedroom door shut before he could block it with his foot. I spent the rest of the afternoon locked in my room. Now that my fighting days are over, I'm constantly trying to find things to tease him about. To me the ringworm was heaven-sent.

"I would have liked to see him. It's been a while." Auntie Esther reaches into her handbag.

"Here's something for you to share with your brother." She presses some notes into my palm. I stand and thank her with a curtsey, then I sit down again. Conscious of my mother's eyes boring into me, I made sure I don't look at the money though I am dying to count it.

Auntie Esther's smile is plastic, my mother's is genuine, and for good reason: my performance so far is impeccable.

"How is school?" Auntie Betty asked the dreaded question. Experience has taught me to hesitate before responding to Auntie Betty's questions. Just in case my mother feels the need to cut in with a more appropriate answer.

"Wandi is doing very well in school. She came top of the class last term," my Mother replies as I anticipated. I don't consider coming twelfth in a class of thirty-five top of the class but I know better than to voice my opinion.

"Well done! Give me five." Auntie Betty holds out her palm and I clap mine against it.

Then I cross my fingers and hope for a change of subject.

"How is Wandi's father?" Auntie Betty comes to my rescue and moves on. She has a long list of our household occupants to run through.

"He's very busy, you know how it is being a doctor." My mother never fails to remind Auntie Betty, or any one else for that matter, of my father's occupation. "The clinic recently extended its opening hours and he's still works at the hospital two days a week."

Although I'm not looking at my mother, I detect her hesitation. I know the subject has unnerved her. It's brought unpleasant memories flooding back. My stomach churns too in anxiety. It's a feeling I've lived with for the two months now, since my father left us.

"I mentioned to him that you would be passing through today and he asked me to give you his greetings and apologies that he's unable to be here." My mother tries to sound normal but I know in a flash that, like me, she relived our recent experience.

MY FATHER

My father is a quiet man. A tall, lanky figure, he waltzes around the house in a world of his own. The rare times he's home, he confines himself to his bedroom where he listens to his radio or his reggae music while browsing through his medical books. Although he loves being a doctor, I know his first love is music. Sometimes he takes out his guitar and strums a few tunes. Whenever he does, his face radiates contentment. It's a look that I've never seen on his face at any other time. Before he studied medicine he wanted to be a composer. When he told his father of his ambitions he was banned from singing and playing the guitar.

"My father thought that my love of music would distract me from studying medicine," my father once explained his father's motives to me. "In a way I understand how he felt. A music career would not have got me where I am today," my father said wistfully. Somehow he didn't look as convinced as he tried to sound. My father is a simple man. He would have been happy singing his way through life. He doesn't look like a doctor; in fact, he doesn't look like a dad either. Whenever I introduce him to my friends for the first time they look surprised. I can understand why. Once you've seen my mother, well-groomed and sophisticated, my father looks out of place beside her. My mother is conscious of my father's appearance and I sympathize with her. She puts so much effort into everything she does, whereas my father puts little effort into anything, except his work and his music.

As soon as you walk into our house you're met with a big black and white portrait of my parents on their wedding day. It hangs on the hall wall directly opposite the front door. They're smiling as they stare into one another's eyes, champagne glasses touching in a toast. Apart from my mother having doubled in size and a few grey hairs on my father's head, they haven't changed much physically. But they've changed on the inside. I hardly see them talk to one another nowadays, let alone smile. My father is always at work. My mother also works but she's home more often. When she's not working all her time is taken up with running the home and keeping everyone in the household in order. Any time they do have together my mother spends nagging my father. She nags about his unkempt look. His lack of ambition. His love of music. My father responds by turning up his radio. He doesn't say anything. At least he didn't until about two months ago, when he made his point.

****

It was after dinner. Beauty and I were washing the dishes in the kitchen. We could hear my mother grumbling about something to my father. But that was such a regular occurrence no one took any notice of what she was saying. Suddenly Junior burst into the kitchen and slammed the door behind him. Beauty turned to tell him off but the look on his face stopped her.

"Junior, what's the matter?" She asked.

"Daddy is shouting." Junior's eyes expressed his fear. We tried to digest Junior's words. It was hard to imagine my father raising his voice.

"What did you do?" Beauty asked.

Before he could reply, we heard a door open and close noisily. Foot steps sounded through the hall and out of the front door. My mother's loud voice drifted through: "Get out of my house! Get out!" We heard her stomp back to her room and slam the door.

My stomach churned with fear and anxiety. I had never seen my parents fight openly. I could still hear my mother hysterically shouting insults through her bedroom window. Beauty and I stood still in the kitchen not knowing what to do. Junior was hunched in a corner behind the kitchen door. He covered his ears with his hands as if to shut out what was happening.

Footsteps sounded on the gravel outside the kitchen window

"Wandi!" I recognized my Uncle George's voice. He was my father's brother. "Come out with Junior. Your father wants to speak to you."

I took hold of Junior's hand and we walked out to my father's car. My father was angry. I could tell because he was breathing heavily. He stammered as he spoke.

"I'm going away. I'll come and see you on Saturday."

His words were brief but he struggled to get them out because he was shaking with anger. A few minutes later he raced down the drive, leaving Uncle George, Junior and me waving dejectedly.

My father was gone for two weeks. He came on the Saturday as he promised and took Junior and me out for the day. We had a nice time. My father was calm and relaxed, which worried me considerably. I thought that if he was happy away from home, he would stay away for ever. Junior and I were on our best behavior; although we didn't discuss the matter, we were both trying to entice my father to come back home.

For the two weeks my father was away my mother was a different woman. She hardly spoke and she walked around looking lost. Everyone in the house tip toed around her while each of us tried to figure out what our fate would be if my parents split for good. It was a thought I tried hard not to contemplate. However, ever so often it crossed my mind. Each time my stomach churned with anxiety.

The day after my father came back, I woke up to the sound of a radio being tuned. The familiar sound spread a warm feeling through me. Just then my mother banged on our bedroom door shouting, "Wake up! Girls shouldn't stay in bed this late!" I smiled to myself. My father was back home. And in a way, so was my mother.

****

My father's brief absence had a profound effect on my mother and me. He scared her by showing that he had limits. And me? After the initial shock of it all, I was proud of him. He proved that he wasn't the walkover my mother had convinced me he was.

COMING OF AGE

I suddenly realise the talking has stopped. The two aunties and my mother are looking at me. I have missed Auntie Esther's question.

"Your grandmother is asking if you have come of age," my mother says.

My mouth dries and my heartbeat quickens. How could I have overlooked the fact that since Auntie Esther's last visit I had started my monthlies? I stare pleadingly at my mother, willing her not to tell the story. If she does I am sure I will die of embarrassment.

****

Six months earlier, Leah called me through the fence that separated my garden from hers. I squeezed through the hole at the bottom of the fence and through the mulberry trees.

"Hurry, we have to go across the road," Leah said excitedly. She was walking away before I straightened up on her side of the fence. "Today Suzyo and Martha are coming out of the house to mark the end of their initiation."

Suzyo and Martha were twins that lived in Matelo. Today was the grand finale of their initiation ceremony. Having been confined indoors for a week, today they were to emerge from the house to declare their womanhood. Beauty had filled me in about menstruation and initiation ceremonies. Except that I wasn't sure what to believe because she tended to exaggerate.

"You'll start yours soon," Beauty said to me one day.

"How do you know?" I asked apprehensively. I didn't like the idea of leaking for seven days every month for the rest of my life. That's how Beauty put it.

"I know because your breasts are starting to grow."

I looked down at my chest. Beauty was right. I had noticed my breasts had started to grow. In the past, Leah and I would pick little green leaves off a plant Beauty had shown us which grew at the bottom of Leah's garden. We would rub the leaves into our breasts. For an hour or so our breasts did seem to grow, but before long they were flat again. Nowadays I didn't need the leaves.

"How will I know the day I'm going to start?" I asked Beauty.

"You won't." Beauty was enjoying my apprehension. Normally I would have stopped there and not given her the satisfaction of scaring me. But I was desperate for answers.

"What if it happens when I'm not at home?"

"Then it happens."

"So the first time it comes without warning!"

"Not only the first time. Every month it starts unannounced."

"How much?"

Beauty opened the kitchen sink tap she was standing by to a continuous dribble.

I stared at her in disbelief.

"It's true! But don't worry too much, just remember every female has them. You'll manage."

I had lots more questions but decided against asking in case I didn't like the answers. Besides, I had enough on my plate trying to figure how to best prepare myself for the imminent arrival of womanhood.

That's why I was so interested in Suzyo and Martha's initiation. They were the first of my friends to be initiated. I trailed Leah across the main road and the ditch. We raced between the houses and across the school playing field. Momentarily I remembered I had left home without covering my tracks. Although my mother didn't say so openly, I know she doesn't approve of my friendship with Leah. I suspect it's because Leah's father is a house-help. He works for the white couple who live next door to us. Leah's mother sells tomatoes in the market. Leah is only a year older than me but because her parents are always out she looks after her her younger brothers. The youngest one is still a baby so Leah ties him on her back with a cloth while we play.

Every day, before her mother returns from the market, Leah sweeps the compound surrounding their two roomed house. She baths the baby and two of her other brothers under the outside tap. Then she lights the charcoal pot ready for her mother to cook when she returns from the market. It's a lot of work. I often help Leah with her chores. At times my mother spots me through the fence with Leah's baby brother on my back. She doesn't have to say anything. Her disapprovingly glare says it all.

The sound of drumming met our ears as we approached the crowd that had gathered outside the twins' house. A makeshift stage had been constructed from flat sheets of timber held up by thick wooden beams.

"That is where they will dance," Leah explained. "They have to be on top so everyone can see them."

"When will they go back to school?" I was amazed at the fact that the twins' parents had allowed their children out of school for a whole week.

"They will go back to school when the whole process is finished. Now they are women they have to learn how to behave as such." Leah seemed to see nothing wrong with the girls being kept from school.

Loud applause from the crowd interrupted our conversation. Leah took my hand and ducked through the crowd. I followed close behind. Leah knew her way around Matelo. With her I felt safe. Leah wasn't scared of the tough children of Matelo who thrived on settling all confrontations with their fists. She was tough and didn't hesitate to prove it. With her head always clean-shaven - her school didn't allow children to grow their hair- and her bow legs, she looked like a boy. If her stories were anything to go by, she fought like one. Her hands and feet were hard and chapped. She once stepped on me accidentally with her bare feet, the pain was no different to the time Uncle George stepped on my foot with his school cadet boots.

We maneuvered to the front of the crowd and climbed a tree that was situated close to the make shift stage. I climbed up the tree after Leah with ease. We often sat in this tree when we played at the twins' house.

"Here they come!' Leah shouted. Suzyo and Martha emerged from their house, lead by a girl slightly older than them. The crowd roared and the drumming intensified.

The girls were covered in reddish-brown clay from head to toe. Even their hair was matted in clay. Around their necks, colourful beads of varying lengths hung down to cover their breasts. Matching beads adorned their waists, wrists and ankles. The drumbeat and cheers rose as the girls mounted the stage and faced their audience. On cue from the older girl, Martha and Suzyo started to move. The tempo of the drums was slow and the girls moved slowly. Holding their hands up, they turned them inwards and outwards to the rhythm of the beat. The tempo increased gradually in sync to the dance movements. At full tempo the girls shook their waists from side to side, their short straw skirts tossed wildly from side to side.

Then they dropped to their knees and gyrated their hips in circular motion. Notes and coins rained onto the stage as the crowd showed their appreciation. The older girl leading the dance collected the coins in jar. She picked up notes and attached them to the girls' waists and head bands. Before long they were covered in notes.

Suzyo and Martha's mother joined her daughters in the dance, her face glowed with pride. The drummers' bodies glistened with sweat as they responded to the atmosphere. It was so electrifying I got goose bumps all over my body!

****

"Are Suzyo and Martha any different now?" I asked Leah the day after the initiation.

"They're the same," Leah replied, eyeing me oddly. I knew she thought I was naïve but curiosity got the better of me.

"Did they tell you what they did to them during the week they were confined?"

"I didn't ask because I know that they aren't allowed to tell. But I know what they were told," Leah smiled slyly. She looked around to make sure no one was listening, then whispered,

"They were told not to play with boys anymore because they are women now. They were also taught how to behave like women. How to respect their bodies, and keep them clean, so they don't smell." Leah finished her sentence by turning up her nose as if something smelt foul.

"It took seven days to tell them that!"

"Sometimes it takes longer."

We sat quietly for a while. So far what Leah told me corresponded to what Beauty had told me.

"Will you have an initiation ceremony when you start?" I was still curious.

"If my father can afford it I will. If not I'll go to my grandmother for a while. It's cheaper to have it in the village." Leah hesitated a moment then asked, "Will you?"

"I hope not. I think it's embarrassing to let everyone know"

Leah looked surprised but didn't say anything. Although she and I were good friends, in many ways we were worlds apart. We were both well aware of our vast differences. But we chose to ignore them, rather than try to reconcile them.

"I know for a fact my parents wouldn't pull me out of school for a week," I said. As I expected Leah didn't comment. "When you go to your grandmother's will you tell me everything?"

"Of course I will. I'm older than you so I'll start first and I'll tell you everything."

Two months later Leah came of age. She didn't have an initiation ceremony because her father couldn't afford one. However, her father bought her two new dresses, two pieces of cloth and a new blanket. Her grandmother sent her some bright coloured beads which she shared with me. We sat down the day she got them and threaded two strings each. Mine were green, yellow and white. Leah's were red, blue and white. I wasn't sure of my mother's reaction to my wearing beads around my waist so I didn't say anything to anyone. Not even Beauty. But two weeks after I wore them my mother walked into the bathroom when I was having a bath.

"Where did you get those from?" She gaped.

A few seconds later when I figured out what she was gaping at, I told her. It was one of the few times I've seen my mother lost for words. Later that evening, Granny-ma came and cut them off my waist without much explanation. All she said was, "I'll keep them for you, till you're older." I didn't probe. Beauty had already briefed me.

I didn't tell Leah Granny-ma had confiscated my beads. I didn't want to disappoint her. She was usually on the receiving end of our friendship and I knew she had taken pleasure in giving me something for a change. Not that she would have noticed, she was preoccupied with coming of age. Although I couldn't understand why Leah was so pleased about something I was dreading, her reaction made me less apprehensive. I found myself thinking maybe I had nothing to fear.

As it happened when 'D' day arrived I was caught totally unawares.

MY TURN

I was in Matelo market helping Beauty spend her pay-packet. We were so engrossed in admiring the colourful fabrics and hair accessories in the various stalls we didn't notice the sun disappear behind the clouds.

Suddenly the smell of rain filled the air and deep grey clouds gathered menacingly in the skies.

"We had better hurry." Beauty wrapped her merchandise tightly in a plastic bag and quickened her pace. I hurried along beside her. A feeling of dread settled in the pit of my stomach. I regretted disobeying my little voice. I had come to the market against my mother's rules. Even worse, I was wearing the new red canvas shoes that had arrived the previous day from Auntie Aggie. There was no way my mother would have allowed me to wear them until a special occasion arose. But I couldn't wait. And since my mother had forgotten to lock them away in her room after I tried them on, I decided to wear them to the market. My little voice objected. But I argued it was only for a few hours. I would clean them and put them back where I had found them later.

Beauty and I ducked simultaneously as lightening flashed across the sky followed by a roar of thunder. We broke into a run.

"Maybe we should shelter under one of the stalls until it stops!" I called to Beauty. We had slowed to a brisk walk.

"No! We have to get home."

She sounded scared. I wasn't sure if it was the storm or the possibility of the rain holding us up and my mother discovering we had been to the market.

"Lightening is dangerous - we could get struck!" My fear of lightening gave me the courage to challenge Beauty. I was also frightened of my mother getting home before us. However, I figured whatever the consequences of her finding out we had been to Matelo were, they paled in significance to the consequences of being struck by lightening.

"If we hurry, we'll get home before the rain starts." Beauty clutched her plastic bag to her chest and started to run again.

"It's coming!" I shouted. The rain roared up from behind and swept past, leaving us drenched through within seconds. I could make out Beauty ahead of me but I could see nothing else. We dashed out of the market and across the school field.

"Don't stop!" Beauty called back to me. I didn't reply; my soaked clothes and water logged canvas were weighing me down. I watched Beauty slide around in the mud, her flip-flops creating suction against the ground. Eventually she gave up, pulled them off and raced off into the distance.

"Slow down! We're already wet." A sharp pain pierced my side.

Beauty didn't hear me. I splashed through the puddles as fast as I could. By the time we crossed the school field, the rain had subsided as abruptly as it had started. We crossed the road that doubled as our playground and headed for the main road. Beauty stopped suddenly as she approached the big ditch. I heard the water before I saw it. The two of us stared helplessly ahead. Muddy rain water was gushing through the ditch like a fast-flowing river. Only one wooden plank remained of the make shift bridge. It balanced dangerously across the ditch which had been widened by the water.

"We can't cross." I stated the obvious. Or so I thought until I saw the look on Beauty's face.

"We can." Beauty gave the response I feared but anticipated.

"How?"

"You get on my back and we'll wade across. I'll hold onto the pole on the other side so we can climb up. Take your shoes off," Beauty instructed.

I stalled. Granny-ma always warned me against playing in rain water without shoes.

Her words rang out in my ears.

"You'll get very sick if you play in rain water without your shoes! You'll get bilharzia and end up with blood in your urine."

"Hurry!" Beauty urged me on. She hunched her shoulders and offered me her back. "Jump on!"

"I'll get sick if I take my shoes off. Let's just take the long way home," I pleaded.

"Wandi, do you want to get me into trouble with your mother?"

"She'll only shout at you."

"You know what she's like. She'll scream for hours. She'll even bring up incidents that happened last year. We're going to get home before her because we're going to cross this ditch now!"

Beauty was determined.

Sensing my reluctance she changed tactics. She tried blackmail.

"If I get into trouble with your mother, I'll tell her about Mr Paulo's mangoes".

I was trapped. The day before, Leah, Isaac her younger brother and I had jumped over the wall into a neighbour's garden and taken some mangoes from his trees. Mr Paulo is a mean-looking old white man. Apparently he doesn't like children, particularly black ones. Rumour has it he came from his country with his family, but they left him behind when they went back after independence because he's so cruel. Because he's so unfriendly, my mother warned us to stay away from his property. However, every rainy season his ripe yellow mangoes beckoned tantalisingly at us from across the wall. That day we couldn't resist them. The three of us scrambled over and grabbed as many mangoes as we could fit into our pockets. We clambered back over the wall and landed right in front of

Leah's mother. She sent me home immediately. I went straight to the kitchen sink to wash my mangoes. But before I could start my feast, Leah and Isaac's screams for mercy as their mother lashed them with a stick from the mulberry tree drifted through the window. The mangoes immediately lost their appeal. So I offered one to Beauty but she didn't help by saying she didn't eat stolen food. So the mangoes ended up in the bin. Now just as I thought I had gotten away with my misdeed, Beauty threatened to give me up.

****

She hunched her back to me again. I jumped on without further protest. With my eyes tightly shut, the noise of the gushing water was even more menacing. At least Beauty had allowed me to keep my shoes on. I latched onto her tightly as she waded across the ditch. I could feel the water up to my waist. I felt the tension in Beauty's body as she reached for the rusty pole that was once part of the fence. Just as she heaved us up onto the other side of the ditch she slipped. I heard her gasp just before I splashed backwards. The muddy water filled my mouth. Gripped with panic I kept hold of Beauty. My arms had slipped from around her neck but I clung desperately to her waist. Beauty regained her balance and managed to grab hold of the pole at her second attempt. She hoisted us up onto the other side and squealed with delight.

Then she saw the expression on my face. I was staring back at the water. She followed my gaze and was just in time to see one of my brand new shoes being swept away by the current.

We paddled home in silence, cold, wet and scared. Even the sight of an empty car port, indicating that my mother wasn't home yet, did little to lift our spirits. The little voice in my head chanted, "I told you so" repeatedly.

I headed straight for the bathroom and peeled off my muddy clothes. I sat on the toilet and tried to figure out how I would explain the disappearance of my shoe to my mother.

As I got up to flush the toilet I peered into the bowl and stopped dead in my tracks . This had to be the worst day of my life. I had caught Bilharzia!

****

My mother had promised not to tell anyone I had mistaken my transformation to womanhood for Bilharzia. But as I stare at her in the presence of her aunties, I'm not sure she will keep her promise.

"Yes, she has." As I'm taking ages to respond, my mother replies for me. "And she's coped very well."

I exhale. My mother isn't going to sell me out after all. She actually looks and sounds proud of me. If I could, I would walk over and kiss her.

"Are you going to hold an initiation ceremony for her?" Auntie Esther asks, deflating the euphoria that has welled up inside me.

"Her father said it wasn't necessary." My mother uses my father as a shield against criticism from her aunties. She knows they disapprove of the fact that I'm not going to be initiated into womanhood. But they can't openly criticize or speak against any of my father's decisions because he is an in-law and the code of behavior between in-laws demands that they always show the utmost respect towards one another.

I watch Granny-ma with my father. They live under the same roof but spend their time avoiding one another. Maybe it's just as well my father is never at home. Granny-ma is so much more relaxed when he's away. When my father comes from work, as a matter of routine the first thing he does is seek out Granny-ma. To make his life easier, Granny-ma settles in her usual place under the mango tree in the back yard when she hears his car come up the drive. My father doesn't walk right up to her because they have to maintain some personal space. He walks to within a few feet of her, bows slightly and calls out his greeting. Granny-ma, regardless of her mood, immediately kneels down, smiles from ear to ear and greets him back. That's the only time of the day they communicate. The rest of the time they seek then hide away from one another.

My mother's tactic works. The two women exchange a knowing look but say nothing. No doubt my lack of initiation will be a topic of discussion on their way home.

The sound of tinkling glass approaches. Beauty stands in the door way holding a tray filled with bottled drinks and glasses.

"Hello Auntie Betty. It's been a long time!" Beauty strolls in and places the tray on the centre table. She kneels down to rearrange the contents of the tray. It's rude to stand before elders so I understand why Beauty is kneeling. But looking at her fat black thighs protruding beneath her short pleated skirt I can't help wondering if she should have remained standing. Auntie Betty glares disapprovingly at Beauty, who doesn't seem to notice. My mother does.

"Beauty, its okay leave the tray, Wandi will serve the drinks," she says. As soon as Beauty leaves the room my mother comments, "Beauty has changed a lot since she came, hasn't she?"

"She's grown. She's changed a lot," Auntie Esther agrees. So do I. The three women look deep in thought for a moment, as though contemplating Beauty's dramatic change. I keep quiet because I know what's changed Beauty from the naïve girl that arrived from the village two years ago to a confident young woman who runs our household like she owns it.

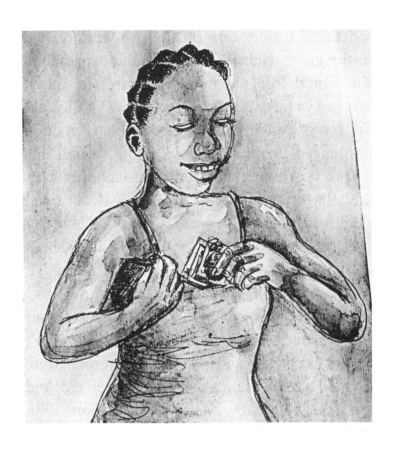

BEAUTY

Two years ago I came home from school to find a young girl sitting at the kitchen table. It's normal in our household for visitors to turn up unannounced and so I waited for my mother's usual long introduction. She always went into a detailed explanation of how we were related to the guest. Half way through the explanation she would lose me though I didn't let on. It was easier and quicker to pretend I followed. So I was caught off guard when my mother introduced Beauty just by saying, "Wandi this is Beauty. Your Granny-da has brought her from the village to help us in the house. Beauty will share your room with you."

Then she continued briefing Beauty about our household.

Meanwhile, I stared at the girl at the table. I had never seen anyone so dark. Beauty's hair was cropped so close to the scalp that if it wasn't for her big bosom and my mother's introduction, I would have mistaken her for a boy. She looked fresh out of a bath; her black face shone with freshly applied Vaseline. I recognized the dress she was wearing as my mother's. I realized Beauty was studying me as intently as I was her. Our eyes met and she smiled revealing a set of perfect white teeth. I smiled back. When my mother finished giving Beauty a run down of the chores she would be expected to do, she left the kitchen. Beauty and I were left alone to get acquainted.

It didn't take Beauty long to settle in our household. In a short time, she discarded her old image. My mother changed her wardrobe. With the help of skin-lightening cream that she kept hidden from my mother, she's now many shades fairer. Beauty even grew her hair. Every week she insisted on washing and stretching my hair with a hot comb. As soon as she did mine, she would wash and stretch hers. I knew Beauty was doing my hair only so that she could do her own but I didn't say anything. Beauty had quickly become the leader of the children in our household. She dished out orders that we carried out with precision. If we got anything wrong she might get into trouble with my mother and Beauty was petrified of my mother. Only in her presence did the old insecure Beauty reappear.

****

Beauty was sixteen when she came to stay, though she seemed much older.

"If I had stayed in the village I would be married by now," she told me one evening as we lay in the darkness of our room. "Just before I left, my grandfather was talking about finding me a husband," Beauty whispered. My mother had banned us from talking late into the night.

"Was he going to choose one for you?" I asked.

"Yes someone in a position to look after me and my family."

I knew she was telling the truth though I felt she was too young to get married. Beauty was only four years older than me but she knew so much. Late at night she told me many stories, most of which I instinctively knew not to repeat to my mother, or any other adult for that matter.

But despite all Beauty told me, I was unprepared for the bombshell she dropped on me one evening as we sorted the laundry.

"Can you keep a secret?" she asked.

"Of course," I replied eager to hear it.

"Uncle Mark said he will marry me."

When her words sunk in I gaped at her in disbelief.

"It's true! I'll soon be your auntie!" Beauty read my expression and tried to convince me.

"What about Auntie Siliza?" I asked; unnecessary question. There was no way my uncle was going to marry a house-help. I didn't voice my thoughts to Beauty. I didn't want to hurt her feelings. I knew she hated being called a house-help.

"I'll be his second wife!" Beauty smiled smugly.

"Are you sure that's what he said?"

"Look," Beauty fished some notes out of her bra cup. "He gave me some money to buy myself something nice."

"Beauty you'll get into serious trouble if my mother or Granny-ma find out!"

"How will they find out?" Beauty's tone was suddenly threatening,

"I won't tell my mother. But I think you should."

"Wandi, your mother will chase me away."

I knew she was right. My mother would send Beauty packing if she found out.

"Then what will you do? What Uncle Mark is doing is wrong."

"Nothing."

"Beauty!"

Both of us were quiet for a while then Beauty spoke. "You don't understand. I need the money to send to my mother. You are lucky you have a mother and father who give you everything. My younger brothers and sisters are relying on me for school fees and uniforms."

"It's just hard to imagine Uncle Mark doing such a thing. Granny-ma and my mother would be shocked if they found out," I said.

Uncle Mark is a short, bald, jovial man. He has a thick moustache and a big tummy that shakes when he laughs. Uncle Mark makes fun of his baldness: he says all the hair meant for his head ended up on his upper lip. Whenever he visits us the whole household is genuinely pleased to see him. He's a likeable person, Granny-ma says that's why he gets away with what he does. You see, Uncle Mark has a weakness for women. He often comes to visit with an Auntie none of us has ever met. His behaviour embarrasses my mother and Granny-ma. My mother tries to tell him off but he brushes her off playfully and does it again. I don't know why my mother bothers; Uncle Mark will never change. Besides, she has more to complain about when he comes to visit with his wife, Auntie Siliza. In contrast to Uncle Mark, Auntie Siliza never smiles, not even when she's around children. I get the impression she doesn't like my mother because she hardly comes to visit. Judging from my mother's comments about Auntie Siliza the feeling is mutual

"Your daughter-in-law should at least try to smile for your benefit," my mother commented to Granny-ma one day after Uncle Mark had paid a fleeting visit with Auntie Siliza.

Granny-ma who never takes sides, replied, "Would you smile if you were married to someone with Mark's bad habits?"

My mother didn't answer.

My silence made Beauty uneasy. She eyed me suspiciously and wagged her index finger at me.

"Wandi, this is a secret. If it ever gets out, I'll know it's you." She switched the iron socket off and walked out with a pile of ironed clothes. I carried on pairing the socks. I felt let down. I knew Uncle Mark had faults but I didn't expect him to take advantage of Beauty. I pondered over what to do. No matter how I looked at it there was no way I could tell someone without getting Uncle Mark and Beauty into trouble. By the end of the day I had decided to keep quiet. I felt guilty because my little voice asked me to tell someone but I couldn't. I contemplated cornering Uncle Mark and asking him to stop. But I couldn't find the guts to do it. When he smiled at me I couldn't believe he would do such a thing. But then again, I believed Beauty. So I ignored my little voice and shut the whole thing out of my mind. Beauty must have sensed my dilemma because she never mentioned Uncle Mark again. She didn't have to. Her change in character and the money she had at her disposal whenever Uncle Mark came to town was a constant reminder. So that's why I wasn't surprised when Beauty waltzed into the room and greeted the guests with such familiarity. As far as she was concerned she was now family!

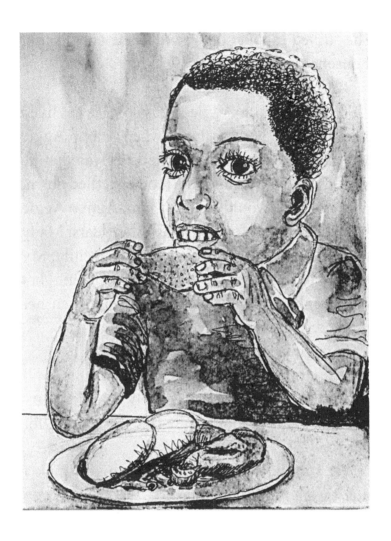

SANGU AND UNCLE GEORGE

Auntie Betty, briefly distracted by Beauty's performance, keeps quiet for a moment before she asked about the next occupant in our household.

"How is Sangu?"

Sangu is Auntie Aggie's only son. He has lived with us since he was three, when Auntie Aggie went to England. The arrangement was that he would stay with us until his mother settled down, and then she would send for him. Auntie Aggie has been trying to settle for over ten years. Many people think Sangu is my parents' first child. My mother has brought him up as her own child but I know she feels her elder sister has taken her granted.

"Sangu is fine," says my mother.

"Have you heard from Aggie?"

Before my mother can reply Auntie Betty asks another question. "When is she coming for her son?"

"If I asked that question, she might think I don't want him in my house."

"That's not the point. Aggie can't expect you to take on her responsibilities for ever. You have done your bit. She ought to take a decision one way or another." Auntie Betty stops to tighten the scarf on her head before she carries on.

"Either she takes him to England or she comes back here."

"Exactly," pipes Auntie Esther. "Not only has she been unfair to you by lumbering you with her son. She had also alienated herself from him. Valuable time in their relationship has been lost. The longer they stay apart the more difficult it will be to bridge the gap."

Auntie Betty, who has been nodding in support of Auntie Esther, adds, "I can't understand what is so special about England. After all, from what I hear, she cleans offices, bars and toilets seven days a week. If that's what she wants in life, fair enough. But she should come for her luggage."

"What money is she still trying to make that she hasn't made in ten years?" Auntie Esther sniggers. Auntie Betty and my mother laugh.

If I didn't know better, I would say something in support of Auntie Aggie at this point. I can't remember her personally but I speak to her often enough on the phone to like her. Besides, whenever she freights a box of things for Sangu she includes clothes for our whole household. All my church and party clothes that my mother keeps locked in her wardrobe are from

Auntie Aggie. The floral blouse and denim skirt my mother is wearing, even the wig on her head, come compliment of Auntie Aggie. But I can't say anything. It's rude to join in an adult conversation. It's even worse to join in and challenge an adult conversation so I keep quiet. Instead I cross my middle and index finger and hope Sangu isn't nearby listening to the conversation. He's very quiet by nature. It's difficult to tell what he's feeling or thinking at any one time. I often wonder if he misses his mother. Sangu's father is a mystery. No one ever talks about him. After a few awkward silences when I asked about his father when I was younger, I got the message. Now I'm old enough to know that I shouldn't ask about things I'm not told about, I just suffer in curious silence.

"I really don't mind raising him, he's my son." I know my mother speaks sincerely; she loves Sangu.

"Why of course," Auntie Betty exclaims "Your sister's child is your child!"

At that moment I wonder how Auntie Betty would react if I asked her why she hadn't raised my mother like her own child. I'm sure if she had, my mother wouldn't suffer from an inferiority complex. That's what Auntie Natasha once told me my mother's problem was.

****

The awkward silence that follows has me thinking I'm not the only one thinking along these lines.

Auntie Betty quickly breaks the silence. "Is he still living with you?"

Although no name is mentioned, we all know who she's talking about. Uncle George is the youngest in my father's family. He's lived with us almost the same length of time as Sangu. Uncle George is a sore point between my parents' families. My mother is convinced Granny-da sent him to live with us when she realised Sangu had come to stay.

Apparently Granny-da turned up unexpectedly one day with Uncle George and announced that he was to attend the primary school down the road from where we lived. She left without any further explanation. I was too young to recall what happened at the time. But from the way my mother still fumes about it, maybe it's just as well.

"He's still here." My mother answers Auntie Betty's question.

"Where can he go?" Auntie Esther sneers. "His mother can't provide him with a home like this." She waved her hands out, as if presenting our sitting room to us.

Uncle George is the clown of our household. Tall, skinny with small eyes, a big nose and equally wide mouth, he's an uglier version of my father. But I have to agree with Granny-ma, Uncle George has such a pleasant personality he's more appealing than my father. When Uncle George isn't talking and laughing he's eating. Uncle George can eat. After every meal he scrapes the leftovers off Junior's plate and eats them. That's after he's had a second helping. So whenever my mother gets into one of her bad moods and starts shouting indiscriminately about the amount of food we consume in our household, I know she's talking to Uncle George.

"Eating! That's what you do best." My mother bangs pots around in the kitchen. "Do you know or care how hard my husband and I work to put food on the table?"

Sometimes when she gets too personal, Granny-ma cautions her. "Tanya, watch what you say," she whispers. "Do you want your in-laws to hear you? You'll cause a lot of trouble if you talk like that."

"I haven't mentioned names," my mother responds, though her change in tone suggests she's taken heed. When my mother shouts, Uncle George and Sangu retreat to their room where they drown my mother's words by playing Sangu's radio cassette.

Uncle George keeps smiling through it all. Everyday he comes in from school with a funny story to tell. Every evening after dinner as we wash up, Uncle George keeps us entertained. His stories, often grossly exaggerated, have us in fits of laughter. Depending on my mother's mood, when we get too loud she interrupts by screaming "Speak English!" from the living room. Silence descends on the kitchen as Uncle George tries to figure out how to translate his story into English and still maintain its humour. My mother's interruption normally serves its purpose and we break up for the night. There's no use carrying on. Beauty would be lost if Uncle George told the story in English. Besides we know the stories wouldn't sound half as good in any language other than our local one. Needless to say, we carry on the next evening where we left off the previous one.

"What annoys me is she didn't have the decency to ask." My mother explains her contention over Uncle George's presence in our household.

"Your mother-in-law obviously brought him here because she felt if her son can look after his wife's relations he might as well look after his own," says Auntie Betty.

"She forgets my hard earned money also comes into this house." My mother is getting agitated. "That woman always implies that Wandi's father would be wealthy if he didn't have to spend his money on my extended family." My mother always referred to Granny-da as that woman.

"She has no reason to say that, Natasha and Kasuli no longer live with you."

Auntie Esther must have regretted her words the moment she uttered them. Auntie Betty glared at her while my mother pretended not to notice. My heart sank at the mention of my mother's youngest brother Uncle Kasuli.

UNCLE KASULI

Granny-ma says a person's personality is formed by innate characteristics and the environment into which they are born. She believes my mother is spoilt because she was the youngest child for so many years. And Uncle Kasuli was spoilt because he was the youngest child so he got everyone's attention. Few would disagree with the fact that Uncle Kasuli was spoilt. However, the reason and manner in which he was spoilt is a matter of continuing debate amongst the family.

From an early age Uncle Kasuli was a problem. He was stubborn and rebellious. He left school at the age of sixteen barely scraping a pass in his school-leaving exams. Getting him to complete his secondary school was such a strain on the family that no one had the energy to motivate him to pursue further studies. He had the opportunities and there were enough role models in the family but it seems that my uncle always had his own agenda. From an early age he took things that didn't belong to him. Every time he paid us a visit something went missing. The items ranged from Uncle George's clothes, to kitchen utensils. Uncle Kasuli's indiscriminate thieving embarrassed my mother. She was constantly explaining to my father where things had gone. Sometimes she accused the house-helps of taking advantage. She said they were taking things and blaming Uncle Kasuli. But it was wishful thinking on my mother's part. She wanted so much for it to be someone else and not her brother.

Despite his quick fingers, Uncle Kasuli was a gentle, soft spoken young man. When confronted with a theft he would break down and confess. He always promised never to do it again. But there was always a next time.

Of all the siblings, my mother had the most patience with Uncle Kasuli. She persevered longer than any of Granny-ma's other children. But even she gave up the day Uncle Kasuli stole her new sewing machine.

My mother banned him from her house for good.

It was traumatic for Granny-ma when she realized my mother had also given up on her son. She tried to plead with my mother on Uncle Kasuli's behalf but my mother had had enough.

"Tanya, how can you stop your brother from entering your house?" I heard Granny-ma ask my mother the day the sewing machine went missing.

"It's painful for me to," my mother explained, "but Ma, I've tried. I've been very patient with him. But he's taken me for granted. Because I've tolerated him the most, I've suffered the most at his hands. Some of the things he's done to me he wouldn't dare do at Mark or Freda's house."

"So are we throwing him out? Are you saying we should forget about him?" Granny-ma spoke softly. Leah and I strained to hear from outside the kitchen window.

"I don't have the solution for Kasuli. Hopefully this harsh treatment will make him come to his senses."

Granny-ma didn't say any more. I knew she was heart broken. After all, for all his faults Uncle Kasuli was her last born son and she loved him.

The last time I saw Uncle Kasuli is fresh in my mind. It was about two months after my mother had banned him from our house. As we drove in from school, we saw a police car was parked outside our gate and a small crowd had gathered. I recognised Uncle Kasuli amongst them. My mother was instructing the guard to keep the gate shut. She was walking way from the gate towards the house. I jumped out of the car and ran to find Granny-ma. I found her sitting on a mat in the back yard, a tray of groundnuts in her lap. She was shelling them slowly as she hummed a hymn. She didn't look up though I knew she knew I was standing there.

"Granny-ma what's happening to Uncle Kasuli?'

Something snapped inside me. I could hear my mother talking to herself inside the house. She didn't reply. A tear rolled down her cheek.

"They can take him away, he's not my problem," she shouted for Granny-ma to hear.

I raced into the house through the kitchen door and almost collided with my mother who was coming outside.

"What's happening to Uncle?" I asked.

"He owes those men money. So they have brought the police here. They want me to pay up or they'll lock him up.

I dropped to my knees and grabbed hold of my mother's skirt. "Please, Ma, pay for him, please."

My mother shook me loose. I still held on to her. "Ma, please don't let the policemen lock him up." My pleading worked because she stopped shouting. I let go of her dress and she walked to her bedroom. I followed her but she slammed the door in my face. So I sat on the floor outside her door and waited. I could hear rummaging around on the other side of the door.

Seconds later she emerged with some money in her hand. She called our security guard and gave him the money. I followed the guard to the gate. As soon as the policeman took the money he shoved Uncle Kasuli to the ground. The crowd dispersed quickly. I was left staring at my uncle. His eyes were red and his lips were dry and chapped. He got up and brushed the dust from his trousers.

"Can I get you anything?" I asked. I felt guilty that the woman who had refused to let him into our house was my mother.

"Cold water to drink," he croaked.

I raced to the kitchen and grabbed an old supermarket plastic bag from a drawer. Granny-ma's pot was simmering on the stove. Without stopping to think, I scooped two spoonfuls of chicken stew from the pot into my school lunch box and placed it in the bag. I opened the fridge and took a loaf of bread, a bottle of drinking water and a bunch of bananas and added them to the bag. I raced back to the gate. When I got there, Uncle Kasuli was walking away. He must have given up waiting. Tears welled up in my eyes as I approached him and I tried hard to hold them back.

"Thank you," he mumbled taking the bag. He managed a faint smile as our eyes met.

My words caught in my throat so I smiled and nodded in response. Then I turned and ran back home to face my mother's wrath.

It was the last time I set eyes on Uncle Kasuli. I spoke to him a few times after that when he called to speak to Granny-ma. He would greet me in a light-hearted manner. Neither of us ever mentioned our last meeting. I wanted to ask him where he was living but I kept putting it off. Then one day I jolted out of sleep. My cotton night dress was drenched in sweat. The light in the hall shone through into our room. Beauty was standing with her ear to the door. Immediately I sensed something was wrong.

"What's happened?" My heat thumped loudly in my chest.

"Shhh!" Beauty put her finger to her lips to hush me.

I could hear my parents' voices in the hall. I

joined Beauty by the door. My father was on the phone.

"Thank you sir. We'll come to the hospital right away." His next words were drowned by my mother's hysteria. "What has happened to Kasuli?" she screamed at my father. I didn't hear my father's response. I didn't need to. I knew from the hollow feeling in my stomach that something bad had happened to my Uncle.

****

After my parents, Uncle George and the watchman left for the hospital, Sangu and Junior came to our room and we sat up trying to put together the bits we had overheard to get a clearer picture of what had happened. We didn't have much to go by because my father just announced that they were going to the hospital and they left. Granny-ma was in her room. She didn't come out all through the commotion. I guess, like me, she sensed something was wrong. I could hear her humming through the wall. I wished I could go and assure her everything was okay. But it wasn't. So I stayed curled up in my bed and listened to her humming solemnly. Eventually I drifted into restless sleep. I was startled awake by the sound of wailing. It was my mother. I leapt out of bed and hurried out towards the crying. When I got to the hall, Granny-ma was entering the hall from the opposite direction. The front door flew open and my father stood helplessly in the doorway. He walked past me like he hadn't seen me and said something to himself that I didn't understand at the time. Granny-ma dropped to her knees and howled. My mother crawled into the hall behind my father. She and Granny-ma held onto one another and sobbed uncontrollably. They were both calling Uncle Kasuli's name. I felt as if I was dreaming. As though I had left my body and was watching everything happen from somewhere far away. Leah's father had heard the crying and rushed over to our house. With the help of the watchman and Uncle George, they began to remove all the furniture out of the hall and the sitting room. They were preparing the house for mourning. Within minutes the two front rooms were bare. Granny-ma and my mother lay huddled together in the corner of the sitting room, exhausted from crying.

Beauty found me outside and explained that Uncle Kasuli had accidentally been beaten to death. Apparently a fight had broken out over a small debt. I felt terrible. Was it anger I felt, or sorrow, or maybe guilt? I had an image in my head of my uncle being battered to death over a small amount of money. Surely he could have come to his family to help him settle the debt. Then I remembered the last time I had seen him and thought, maybe not.

The news of Uncle Kasuli's passing spread quickly. Our house was a hive of activity. My father spent most of his time accepting condolences in person and over the telephone. I don't know how many times I heard him narrate the details of Uncle Kasuli's death.

"We'll know exactly what happened later......
It was a fight......The police are on the case...."

Listening to him I could image the barrage of questions coming his way.

By mid-morning the house started to fill up. Firstly with friends and neighbours who didn't have far to travel, then friends and relatives who had come from further away. Big trucks delivered firewood, food and drinks. The fire wood was needed to cook large enough meals to feed the mourners. It was also needed to light fires to keep the male mourners, who mourned outside, warm throughout the night.

The mourners kept pouring in. They stamped their feet, beat their chests, and rolled on the ground, in apparent grief for Uncle Kasuli. And each time a new batch arrived, Granny-ma and my mother would join them in another round of crying.

A few minutes after they stopped crying, the latest arrivals would join the rest of the mourners in the enthusiastic chattering, eating and drinking that was taking place. Most of them I had never seen before. I doubted they knew Uncle Kasuli. I wondered where all these people were when Uncle needed them. Then my little voice asked me where I had been. The question left me overwhelmed by guilt and grief.

Although Uncle Kasuli was buried two days after he died and most of the mourners left then, our household was in mourning for up to a month. People still came by to pass their condolences. When the month was up, Uncle Kasuli's few possessions were distributed amongst family and close friends, for them to remember him by. I chose a belt he often wore. It hangs on the hook behind my bedroom door. When I first put it there, Beauty tried to remove it, claiming it would bring Uncle Kasuli's ghost to haunt us at night. I refused to take it down. I'm not afraid of Uncle Kasuli's ghost.

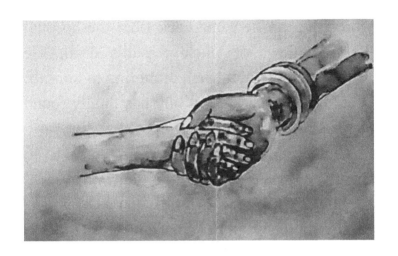

MY MOTHER'S WORDS

An awkward silence falls upon the living room. All three women shifted uncomfortably. Uncle Kasuli's life and death make uneasy conversation. Not just because of the grief of losing him, but more because of the manner in which he died. My mother's family feels guilty in a way. They know people are saying that had Uncle Kasuli not been abandoned, he would still be alive. But those people don't understand the demons that drove my uncle. I always remember my father's words the day he came back from the hospital with the news of Uncle Kasuli's death. He walked past me in the hall muttering to himself. What he said was, "That boy has finally found his peace."

Auntie Betty glances at her wrist watch. Even she doesn't want to delve into the controversial life and death of Uncle Kasuli.

She stretches out her arms and declares, "We have to be on our way now, if we're to get home before dark."

Auntie Esther nods and drains her glass. She doesn't say much. I think she is still embarrassed for bringing up Uncle Kasuli's name. My mother looks relieved that our guests have come to the end of their visit. She can't handle talking about Uncle Kasuli. The memories are too painful. She quickly stands up and thanks the guests for coming.

I stand beside my mother as we wave our guests off. My heart is heavy. Auntie Betty's visit has stirred all kinds of emotions in me. I feel guilty for being better off than Leah and most of the other children in Matelo. I feel guilty because

I don't have younger brothers depending on me for support like Beauty does. I feel bad that my mother doesn't make Uncle George welcome in our house. I even feel selfish for wanting Auntie Aggie to stay in England so I can get new clothes, despite the fact that it robs Sangu of his mother. My mother kept her promise to me and didn't tell Auntie Betty my secret. Meanwhile to date, I continue to swear to her face that I have no idea where my new red canvas shoes are.

Worse still, I feel partly responsible for Uncle Kasuli's death. Why didn't I show that I cared about him? Maybe I should have pleaded more with my mother to give him another chance. But it's too late. No one can help Uncle Kasuli now. Although my mother is standing beside me I feel alone. Even my little voice has gone. Perhaps it's given up on me.

As the car tail lights disappear out of the gate my mother reaches for my hand and squeezes it gently. "Wandi never blame yourself for things out of your control. Sometimes things just happen. There are some things we can change about ourselves but most things we can't."

My mother sighs heavily and leads me to the verandah. She sits on the top step and I sit down beside her.

"For instance, we can't change the family or culture we are born into. We just have to make the most of who we are. No one is perfect. Sometimes we choose not to listen to the voice inside us."

"You have one too?"

"Of course, Wandi! Everyone has a conscience."

My mother's few words lift the heavy weight off my shoulders. Although I haven't spoken, she's sensed my pain and despair. I know she feels the same. She's said the words I needed to hear. Somehow I doubt anyone else could have done that. Suddenly I feel a closeness to my mother I have never felt before. She must feel it too because she puts her arm around me and I rest my head on her shoulder.

We sit quietly for a while. I'm enjoying just sitting close to her but I have some unfinished business.

"Ma, next time Auntie Betty comes to visit can I go out for the day?"

My mother smiles. "Yes you can."

"Thank you." I close my eyes and say my second silent prayer of the day:

"Dear God, Please cancel my earlier request. My real mother is already here with me.

THE END.

Printed in the United States
by Baker & Taylor Publisher Services